Sharkbot Shalom

by Jenna Waldman • illustrated by Sharon Davey

APPLES & HONEY PRESS

To my own little Sharkbots,
who never seem to run out of charge!
—JW

To my cat Eliza—she likes fish.
—SD

Apples & Honey Press
An Imprint of Behrman House Publishers
Millburn, New Jersey 07041
www.applesandhoneypress.com

ISBN 978-1-68115-567-8

Library of Congress Cataloging-in-Publication Data
Names: Waldman, Jenna, author. | Davey, Sharon, illustrator.
Title: Sharkbot Shalom / by Jenna Waldman ; illustrated by Sharon Davey.
Description: Millburn, New Jersey : Apples & Honey Press, an imprint of Behrman House Publishers, [2021] |
Summary: When a shark robot realizes that he is low on charge, he has to rush through Shabbat preparations.
Identifiers: LCCN 2020035447 | ISBN 9781681155678 (hardcover) Subjects: CYAC: Stories in rhyme. |
Sabbath--Fiction. | Sharks—Fiction. | Robots—Fiction. | Marine animals—Fiction. | Jews—Fiction.
Classification: LCC PZ8.3.W145 Sh 2021 | DDC [E]—dc23 LC record available at https://lccn.loc.gov/2020035447

The illustrations in this book were created using hand-drawn line work, which was scanned into the computer
and digitally colored. The artist added found and handmade textures for an authentic look.

Design by Elynn Cohen
Edited by Alef Davis
Printed in China

1 3 5 7 9 8 6 4 2

1021/B1765/A5

Water whirls and bubbles blow
as creatures bustle down below.

Sharkbot sweeps the ocean floor

before his guests swim through the door.

But as he readies for the night—
blink and *buzz* . . . a warning light.

"Slime of snail and tail of trout!
My charge is low—I might run out!"

He scans himself,
then once again—
"Goodness gears,
I'm down to **TEN**!"

There's not much time before Shabbat.
"I should have charged, but I forgot!"

He spins his fins to find the wine.
His charge is slipping down to **NINE**.

Long strands of kelp he's braiding through
give challah loaves a greenish hue.

He sets the table up for **EIGHT**,
a fork and spoon beside each plate.

Whiz and whir,
beep and boop,
Sharkbot stirs the
seaweed soup.

With **SEVEN** hugs, his friends arrive.

They dip and grin, they flip and dive.

The stingray brings **SIX** plates of treats, from seagrass cakes to algae sweets.

The starfish waves **FIVE** arms "Hello!"
The jelly shines her glimmer-glow.

FOUR pufferfish have cooked a dish of plankton pie that looks delish.

He wants to taste a *byte* of food,
but Sharkbot waits—he won't be rude.

Sharkbot's charge descends to **THREE**—
"Tumbling tides, how can this be?"

TWO candlesticks of coral pink . . .

are set down swiftly with a clink!

He motions for his friends to sit.
One final touch and then . . . that's it—

Sharkbot's charge floats down to **ONE**!
He stops. Plugs in. Shabbat's begun.

The current gently ebbs and flows,
and Sharkbot calms from tail to nose.

His friends all share this special night
with words of thanks by candlelight . . .

as into waves of salty foam, the sun sinks low—
SHABBAT SHALOM!

A Note for Families

Shabbat is a time to "recharge our batteries" when the week is through. On Shabbat we slow down, connect with our loved ones, and prepare our minds and bodies for the week ahead. Before Shabbat, Sharkbot feels anxious. But when he has a moment to slow down and focus on the peace that Shabbat brings, a wave of calm replaces his anxiety.

Feeling anxious from time to time is completely normal. For example, you may feel anxious when you're late for school or when you lose something important. Perhaps you use other words to describe the feeling: *worried, nervous, butterflies in your stomach*. However, using your breath and imagination, you can allow anxious thoughts to wash away.

Here is a simple mindfulness exercise that Sharkbot would appreciate.

Try This!

Imagine that you're at the beach. The ocean sparkles before you. Wiggle your toes and let them sink into the cool, wet sand.

Listen to the waves moving in and out, and relax as your breath moves slowly and peacefully with each wave. Take a deep breath in—a wave moves toward the shore. Slowly exhale—the wave retreats to the ocean.

Stand tall like a strand of giant kelp anchored in the sand. Move your shoulders up and down as your arms swing like jellyfish tentacles. Sway from side to side like seagrass. Slowly bend forward so the sun warms your back, bend backward to warm your face, and stand tall again.

Take another deep breath in, let it out, and imagine all of your anxious thoughts being carried away on the tide.